A Note from Michelle about
THE WISH I WISH I NEVER WISHED

Hi! I'm Michelle Tanner. I'm nine years old. And I love birthday wishes. Actually, I like making wishes almost anytime. But I made one wish I really didn't mean. I wished that my sister Stephanie would move out of our room. And she did! But I have a plan to get her to move back. I'm going to throw her a surprise party. The only problem is, I have to keep it a secret from my family. And that's not going to be easy. I live in a *very* full house.

There's my dad and my two older sisters, D.J. and Stephanie. But that's not all.

My mom died when I was little. So my uncle Jesse moved in to help Dad take care of us. So did Joey Gladstone. He's my dad's friend from college. It's almost like having three dads. But that's still not all!

First Uncle Jesse got married to Becky Donaldson. Then they had twin boys, Nicky and Alex. The twins are four years old now. And they're so cute.

That's nine people. Our dog, Comet, makes ten. Sure, it gets kind of crazy sometimes. But I wouldn't change it for anything. It's so much fun living in a full house!

FULL HOUSE™ MICHELLE novels

The Great Pet Project
The Super-Duper Sleepover Party
My Two Best Friends
Lucky, Lucky Day
The Ghost in My Closet
Ballet Surprise
Major League Trouble
My Fourth-Grade Mess
Bunk 3, Teddy and Me
My Best Friend Is a Movie Star!
    (Super Special)
The Big Turkey Escape
The Substitute Teacher
Calling All Planets
I've Got a Secret
How to Be Cool
The Not-So-Great Outdoors
My Ho-Ho-Horrible Christmas
My Almost Perfect Plan
April Fools!
My Life Is a Three-Ring Circus
Welcome to My Zoo
The Problem with Pen Pals
Tap Dance Trouble
The Fastest Turtle in the West
The Baby-sitting Boss
The Wish I Wish I Never Wished

Activity Books

My Awesome Holiday Friendship Book
My Super Sleepover Book

FULL HOUSE™ SISTERS

Two on the Town
One Boss Too Many

Available from MINSTREL Books

FULL HOUSE™
Michelle

The Wish I Wish
I Never Wished

Cathy East Dubowski

A Parachute Book

A MINSTREL® BOOK

Published by POCKET BOOKS

New York   London   Toronto   Sydney   Tokyo   Singapore

A MINSTREL PAPERBACK *Original*

 A Minstrel Book published by
POCKET BOOKS, a division of Simon & Schuster Inc.
1230 Avenue of the Americas, New York, NY 10020

A PARACHUTE BOOK

 Copyright © and ™ 1999 by Warner Bros.

FULL HOUSE, characters, names and all related indicia are trademarks of Warner Bros. © 1999.

ISBN: 0-671-02151-6

First Minstrel Books printing July 1999

10 9 8 7 6 5 4 3 2 1

A MINSTREL BOOK and colophon are registered trademarks of Simon & Schuster Inc.

Cover photo by Schultz Photography

Printed in the U.S.A.

QBP/✶

The Wish I Wish
I Never Wished

Chapter

1

♥ "You know what I like about our family?" nine-year-old Michelle Tanner asked. It was Tuesday. And the Tanner family was eating dinner.

"What?" her father, Danny, asked, putting down his fork.

"Birthdays!" Michelle announced. "With so many people in our family, we get to eat more birthday cake than anybody I know!"

Michelle lived in a very full house. There were her sisters, thirteen-year-old Stephanie and eighteen-year-old D.J., and her father.

Her uncle Jesse and his wife, Aunt Becky, lived on the third floor with their four-year-old twins, Nicky and Alex.

Her dad's best friend, Joey Gladstone, lived in the basement apartment. He moved into the house to help out the family when Michelle's mom died. That was a long time ago. Now he was just like part of the family.

"We have nine birthdays in our house," Michelle pointed out. "That means nine birthday cakes."

"Ten!" Joey corrected her. "You left out Comet!"

Michelle laughed. Comet was their golden retriever.

"And what about your guinea pig, Michelle?" Becky added. "That makes eleven!"

Danny shook his head. "Any excuse to eat cake."

"So, whose birthday is next?" Stephanie asked, pretending not to know.

"Funny, Steph," D.J. said. "You know your birthday is next Tuesday."

Michelle turned to Stephanie. "If you could wish for any birthday cake in the world, what kind would it be?"

Stephanie grinned. "You can't count on wishes. They don't always come true." She looked at Danny. "I'd like a chocolate-chip cake with chocolate icing, please."

Michelle laughed again. She admired her big sister Stephanie, which was good since they shared a bedroom. Michelle was making a special present for her birthday—a bright yellow throw pillow with a ruffle all around it.

"So." Aunt Becky turned to Stephanie. "What do you want for your birthday?"

"Oh, nothing much," Stephanie said with a grin. "Diamonds. Furs. Maybe a little red sports car—with a chauffeur until I'm old enough to drive."

"Hey, that's what I was going to ask for for my birthday," Joey said, pretending to pout.

"That nail polish Darcy and Allie gave you is pretty cool," Michelle said. She scooped up a bite of mashed potatoes. Darcy Powell and Allie Taylor were Stephanie's best friends. "It's so cool that they gave it to you early."

Stephanie placed her fork on the table and glared at her little sister. "How do *you* know what they got me?"

Oops. Michelle froze with a glob of mashed potatoes in her mouth. Slowly she swallowed. "I was looking for a pencil sharpener in your desk," Michelle explained, "and I . . . sort of saw them."

Stephanie frowned. "Did you read the card, too?"

Michelle nodded. "I didn't mean to," she said quickly. "But the front of the card was so funny. I had to look inside to read the rest of the joke."

Stephanie folded her arms. "Can't I have any privacy?" she complained. She turned to Danny. "Dad, can you please tell Michelle to stay out of my things? It's hard enough to have to share a room with a little kid. But it's not fair to have her going through my stuff all the time."

"I wasn't going through your stuff," Michelle protested. "I was just looking for—"

"You were too going through my stuff," Stephanie argued. "I caught you looking in my desk three times this week."

"So what are you hiding in there anyway?" Michelle grumbled.

"Nothing!" Stephanie insisted. "I just want some space that belongs to me. What's wrong with that?"

"Girls!" their father interrupted with a note of warning in his voice. "Let's not argue at the dinner table."

"Sorry," Stephanie mumbled. But she still looked mad.

Michelle didn't like making her sister angry. "I'm sorry, Steph," she told her. "I won't do it again."

"Do you promise?" Stephanie asked.

Michelle made a big *X* over her heart with her finger. "Cross my heart and hope to spit."

Stephanie laughed. "Okay—as long as you don't spit on my half of the room!"

After dinner Michelle hurried up to her room. It was Stephanie's turn to clear the table and load the dishwasher. That would give Michelle some extra time alone.

Michelle closed the door and quickly pulled out a shopping bag from underneath her bed. She took out the yellow pillow she had made for Stephanie's birthday. It sure was hard making a secret present when you shared a room with the person who was getting it!

She checked out the pillow and frowned. This needs something more, Michelle decided. Something special. But what?

Michelle thought and thought.

Glitter paint!

She checked the bottom drawer of her nightstand. That's where she kept a lot of junk, like colored markers and old comic books. She found one tube of glitter paint stuffed in the back. She pulled off the cap and squeezed.

Nothing came out. It was all dried up. With a sigh, Michelle threw the tube in the trash. Now what? She didn't have money to buy new paint.

Then she glanced at Stephanie's desk. She knew her sister had some new glitter paint. And Michelle needed only a little . . .

She looked at the door. Should I do it? she wondered. Even after I promised never to go through Stephanie's desk again?

But this is different, Michelle told herself. This wasn't snooping. This was an emergency!

Michelle dashed across the room. She opened the drawer to Stephanie's desk and stuck her hand inside.

The bedroom door opened with a bang.

"Michelle! What do you think you're doing?" Stephanie cried.

Chapter
2

♥ "Uh . . . hi, Steph," Michelle said, hiding the pillow behind her back.

"Michelle! I can't believe you're snooping in my stuff again!" Stephanie shouted. "We just got through talking. You just promised you wouldn't go through my things!"

Michelle dashed to her bed and stuffed the pillow into the shopping bag. "But I wasn't!"

"Michelle! How can you say that?" Stephanie replied. "I caught you with your hand in my desk drawer!"

9

Michelle tried to explain. "I . . . I just wanted to borrow your new glitter paint."

"What for?" Stephanie asked.

Michelle didn't know what to say. "Um, just . . . something."

"Well, forget it," Stephanie said. She shoved the desk drawer closed. "I need it for school."

"Please?" Michelle begged. "I'll use only a little. I promise."

"Michelle! I said no," Stephanie exclaimed. She pointed toward the door. "Now, go downstairs, okay? Darcy's on her way over. She and I need to talk—in *private*."

Michelle shook her head. "Why do *I* have to leave? It's my room, too."

Stephanie dug around in her desk. "I'll give you some of my old glitter paint if you do." She held out the tubes.

Michelle didn't like getting kicked out of her own room. But she *did* want the paints.

"Okay," she said at last, reaching for the paints. Then she grabbed the shopping bag and headed for the door. "Just don't mess up my side of the room."

Stephanie rolled her eyes and followed Michelle to the door. Michelle stepped out into the hall.

"Tell Darcy to come on up when she gets here," Stephanie ordered.

"Yeah, sure," Michelle mumbled. Then Stephanie slammed the door in her face.

Michelle stuck her tongue out at the door. She had some glitter paint now. But somehow she didn't feel like working on the dumb pillow anymore.

"This is awesome!" Michelle told her best friends, Cassie Wilkins and Mandy Metz, the next afternoon.

It was Wednesday. The girls were in

Michelle's room, making a big map of the world for social studies.

Michelle started coloring France with a purple marker.

Then the door banged open. Stephanie sailed into the room with Darcy and Allie. Their arms were loaded with snacks, sodas, and books.

"Hi, guys," Stephanie greeted them.

"All right!" Michelle cried when she saw the munchies. She reached for a bag of taco chips. "We're starved."

"Sorry, Michelle," Stephanie said, laughing. "These are for us. Go get your own snacks." She dropped her books on her desk. Then she smiled at Michelle and her friends. "We've got a lot of studying to do. So you guys have to go play somewhere else, okay?"

Michelle frowned. "We're not *playing*. And why should we have to leave? We were here first."

"Right," Stephanie argued. "You already had the room to yourselves. Now it's our turn. We've got tons of homework."

Michelle jumped to her feet. "So do we!"

Stephanie glanced at the map on the floor and sighed. "But we have a huge test tomorrow. And it's *real* schoolwork. Our studying is a lot more important than your poster."

"Our poster is just as important as anything you're doing!" Michelle cried back.

"Look, will you guys just get out of here?" Stephanie exclaimed.

Michelle blushed. It was bad enough that Stephanie was kicking her out of their room again. But now she was getting kicked out in front of her friends. How embarrassing!

"But, Stephanie—" Michelle began.

"Uh, come on, Michelle." Cassie started gathering up the art supplies. "Let's go."

"Maybe we can work on the poster on the

kitchen table," Mandy said. "That will give us lots of room to spread out."

Michelle glanced at her friends. They definitely wanted to leave. "Fine," she told Stephanie. "But next time we get the room."

Stephanie smiled. "Sure. Whatever." Then she and her friends started talking, giggling, and eating chips.

Michelle didn't say any more. But she decided to talk to her dad when he got home.

It was different sharing a room when she and Stephanie were little. They played together a lot more back then. But now they were growing up. They needed to work out some better rules for how to share their room.

As soon as Danny came home that night, Michelle ran to talk to him.

"It's not fair!" Michelle complained. "Stephanie thinks just because she's bigger—"

"Whoa, slow down," Danny said, laughing. "I just got home. Let me at least put down my briefcase."

Michelle waited until her father put away his things. Then he sat down on the living room couch with her. "Okay, pumpkin. What's wrong?"

"Stephanie kicked me out of the room in front of Cassie and Mandy," Michelle explained. "Just so she and her friends could study. But I was doing homework, too."

"Well, I know Stephanie had a pretty important test coming up," Danny pointed out.

"But it's not fair, Dad," Michelle went on. "She acts like it's her room."

"It *is* her room," Danny said. "And your room, too."

"But I never have any privacy," Michelle complained.

"I guess Stephanie feels that way, too," Danny replied.

Michelle frowned. "Why are you taking Stephanie's side?"

"I'm not," Danny insisted. He put his hand on Michelle's shoulder. "I know it's tough to share. We have a big family. All of us have to give up a little sometimes to make things work—even the grown-ups. I wish I could just snap my fingers and give you your own room. But I can't. It's a full house."

"But, Dad—"

"I'm sorry, honey," Danny said. He gave her a hug. "I know it's hard. But you and Stephanie will work things out. I'm sure of it."

But Michelle didn't feel like working things out with Stephanie. She didn't say one thing to Stephanie during supper, not even when they had to clear the table together.

The worst part was, Stephanie didn't seem to mind.

After supper Michelle stormed up the

stairs to her room and did her homework. Later she put on her pajamas, then climbed under the covers with a big fat book. She was lost in the story when Stephanie came into the room.

Stephanie banged around, getting ready for bed. Michelle tried not to let the noise stop her from reading.

Then Stephanie turned off the lights and climbed into bed.

"Hey!" Michelle cried, and flicked on her bedside lamp.

"Michelle, turn out your light," Stephanie said. "I've got to get some sleep or I'll flunk my test."

"But I wanted to read—" Michelle protested.

"Then do it somewhere else," Stephanie said. "I should be able to go to sleep when I want to in my own room."

"*Our* room," Michelle pointed out.

"Yeah . . ." Stephanie yawned and turned over. "Whatever."

Michelle flipped her book closed and placed it on her nightstand. Then she turned off the light. But she didn't feel like going to sleep.

Stephanie's acting like she owns the place, Michelle thought. Why should I always have to listen to her just because she's older? It's not fair!

Michelle rolled over and sighed. She gazed out her window at the flickering stars in the sky, and noticed one star that seemed to shine brighter than the others.

I know what I'll do, Michelle thought. She stared at the shining star and made a wish.

"I wish I had a room of my own," she whispered.

Chapter

3

♡ Michelle hummed as she skipped into her room after school the next day. She had a plan. A plan to take control of her share of the room.

She dug out her colored markers, paper, scissors, and a roll of thick white tape from her drawer. Then she began to make some signs.

"Let's see," Michelle said, thinking out loud. Her eyes lit up as she wrote:

DO NOT TOUCH

Excellent, Michelle thought. Then she wrote another one.

FOR MICHELLE'S USE ONLY

This was fun! Her next note was even better.

KEEP OUT—AND THIS MEANS YOU, STEPHANIE!

She drew a little skull and crossbones on that one to make it extra scary.

She was still making signs when Stephanie came home with Darcy. "Hi, Michelle," Stephanie said.

Michelle didn't answer. Instead, she pressed a long strip of white tape down the middle of the bedroom floor—to divide the room in half.

"May I have your attention, please?" Michelle announced. "This is now officially *my* side of the room. That's *yours*. You can't cross the line."

"Oh, brother!" Stephanie said, rolling her eyes.

"Oh, *sister!*" Michelle said back.

Darcy giggled.

"Is this for real?" Stephanie asked.

Michelle smiled. "You bet!"

Next Michelle picked up her small stack of signs. She used tape to stick the signs all over the room.

Stephanie and Darcy giggled.

"This is so lame," Stephanie whispered to her friend.

Michelle pretended not to hear.

"So, Darcy," Stephanie said. "What do you think of my shirt?" She looked at herself this way and that in the mirror over her dresser.

"Is it new?" Darcy asked. "Purple looks great on you."

"Thanks. I got it last weekend at the mall." Stephanie glanced in Michelle's direction. Then her eyes lit up. "That would match perfectly!" She crossed over the white line to

Michelle's side of the room. And scooped up a purple scrunchie from the top of Michelle's dresser. Then she pulled her long blond hair into a ponytail with it.

"Hey!" Michelle cried, grabbing for the scrunchie. "Give that back!"

Stephanie whirled out of her way. "Come on, Michelle," she said. "Let me wear it—please?"

"No way," Michelle said. "It's private property. Hand it over." She stuck out her hand.

"Fine!" Stephanie said angrily. She yanked the scrunchie out of her hair and threw it onto Michelle's dresser. "You want to be selfish? Then I'm taking back the paints I gave you yesterday."

"You can't," Michelle protested. "They're mine now!"

"Not anymore!" Stephanie shouted back.

She darted to Michelle's desk and snatched up the colored tubes.

Michelle tried to grab them out of Stephanie's hand.

"Stop it!" Stephanie cried, pushing Michelle away.

"Gimme!" Michelle said, pulling Stephanie's hands.

The two sisters struggled. Michelle caught hold of a tube of paint and yanked—hard.

Squirt!

The cap popped off.

Michelle froze as a stream of glittery red paint spurted out from the tube. And landed right on Stephanie's brand-new shirt!

Uh-oh.

Chapter

4

♥ "Michelle!" Stephanie yelled. "You *ruined* my brand-new shirt!"

Michelle's hand flew to her mouth. "Oh, Steph! I'm—I'm sorry." She grabbed a bunch of tissues from her desk and tried to wipe the paint off Stephanie's T-shirt.

"Quit it!" Stephanie exclaimed, backing away. "You're making it worse."

"Whoa. That T-shirt is history!" Darcy declared.

"I can't believe it!" Stephanie wailed,

staring into the mirror. "And I just bought it."

Michelle felt her face turn red. Stephanie was acting as if Michelle did it on purpose. "I *said* I was sorry." Then she mumbled, "Even though it *was* your fault."

"*My* fault!" Stephanie said. "That's a joke."

"I don't like sharing a room with you anymore," Michelle cried. "I wish you would just move out!"

"You don't want to share a room with me? You got it!" Stephanie grabbed the pillow and quilt from her bed. "I'm leaving!"

"Leaving?" Michelle said, stunned. "What do you mean?"

"I'll find somewhere else to sleep," Stephanie shouted at her. "Maybe I'll camp out on the couch in the living room. Maybe I'll get Darcy's family to *adopt* me!" She

25

glared at Michelle. *"Anything* is better than sharing a room with *you!"*

Stephanie stormed out of the room.

Darcy stared at Michelle. "Whoa." She popped her bubble gum. "I'm glad I don't have to share a room with *my* sister." Then she followed Stephanie downstairs.

Michelle flopped onto her bed. She sighed and stared at the tips of her pink and blue high-tops. Michelle felt awful for fighting with Stephanie. "I guess I should apologize again," she muttered under her breath.

Then silence filled the room.

And slowly, Michelle began to smile.

She jumped to her feet and pumped her fist in the air. "All *riiight!"* she squealed. "I got my wish!"

Stephanie was moving out. Now Michelle had a room of her own!

She quickly closed the door, then whirled

around, breathless. She looked around her room as if she'd never seen it before.

A room of her very own. Michelle couldn't believe it. What should she do first?

Michelle grabbed an armload of her dirty clothes from the hamper and threw them on the floor—right in the middle of the room.

No Stephanie to say, "Michelle—you're such a pig."

She ran to her desk and turned on her radio— loud! She switched it to the kind of music she liked and began to dance around the room.

No Stephanie to tell her to turn it down or change the station.

Michelle began to jump up and down on her bed.

No Stephanie to say, "I'm going to tell Dad."

Michelle giggled to herself. This is terrific!

"I'm the queen!" she cried. "Queen of my own room!"

Then Michelle's door opened a crack, and her dad popped his head inside. "Uh, Michelle, honey? Could you turn your radio down?" he asked. "Uncle Jesse says the twins are taking a nap."

"Oh. Okay, Dad." Michelle turned down the radio. So what if she couldn't play music as loud as she wanted? She could still play what she liked, when she liked it!

"Oh, and Michelle?" her dad added. "Let's pick those clothes up off the floor. Okay?"

Michelle sighed. "Okay, Dad."

Stephanie ate dinner at Darcy's house that night. So Michelle didn't have to see her.

At bedtime Michelle crawled into bed and opened the book she was reading the night before.

She heard Stephanie come in the front door.

Uh-oh. Has she changed her mind about sharing a room with me? Michelle wondered. She listened carefully. Was Stephanie coming upstairs?

No. Michelle didn't hear anything.

All riiight! Michelle thought. I can read all night if I want to. I can even go to sleep with the light on. Cool!

Soon her dad came into her room. He sat down on the edge of her bed. "I hear you and Steph had a little fight."

"Yeah." Michelle wondered how much her sister had told him. Did she tell only *her* side of the story? Was Michelle in big trouble?

"Do you want to talk about it?" he asked gently.

Michelle shook her head. "Not really."

Her dad sighed. He looked as if he was going to say something else. But then he seemed to change his mind.

"Well, I guess that's part of being sisters," he said with a crooked smile. "I'll be in my room reading, if you change your mind. But I'm sure you girls will work things out tomorrow."

He kissed her good night and tucked her covers up to her chin. He clicked on her blue and pink teddy bear night-light. Then he turned off the lamp. "Good night, pumpkin," he said as he pulled her door closed.

Whew! Michelle thought. That was close. No lecture!

Maybe she and Stephanie would patch things up tomorrow. But Michelle kind of hoped not. Having a room to herself suited her just fine.

Michelle snuggled down into her bed with her favorite stuffed bear, Mr. Teddy.

The room was nice and quiet.

Really quiet.

Maybe *too* quiet!

"I guess I'm used to Stephanie's snoring," she joked to Mr. Teddy. That was the problem with big old houses. The walls were thick and there were lots of rooms. Sometimes it was hard to hear anybody else in the house.

Joey was way, way down in the basement. Uncle Jesse and Aunt Becky were usually way, way up in their attic apartment with the twins. And her dad seemed way, way down the hall.

Michelle fussed with her covers and rolled on to her side.

She closed her eyes, then popped them back open.

Was it darker than usual in her room tonight?

She heard a sound—a sound like a creepy *squeeeeak.*

Michelle sat up in bed. *What was that?* she wondered.

Michelle didn't hear the noise again. Just

the *tick-tock, tick-tock* of the grandfather clock in the hallway.

"Don't worry," she assured Mr. Teddy. "It was nothing."

Michelle lay back down. She pulled the covers up to her chin. She closed her eyes so she couldn't see how dark it was. She hugged Mr. Teddy tight.

Michelle had wished for her own room. And her wish had come true. But there was one tiny thing she had forgotten.

Having your own room meant that you had to sleep in it alone.

All alone.

Her room had never seemed so dark and empty.

Her house had never seemed so old and creaky.

And Michelle never felt so lonely in all her life!

Stephanie would probably laugh at me for being so scared, she thought. But Michelle couldn't help herself. She missed her big sister. A lot.

Then she stared out her window at the starry night sky.

"Do you think you can *un*-wish a wish?" she whispered to Mr. Teddy.

Mr. Teddy looked doubtful.

But Michelle didn't care. She had to try, and so she wished with all her might. "I wish I never wished to have a room of my own!"

Chapter 5

♥ The next morning when Michelle woke up something felt different. Something was wrong.

She glanced at her clock. Seven-fifteen. "I overslept!"

Michelle threw back the covers and jumped out of bed.

Stephanie's bed was neatly made up.

No wonder. Stephanie was usually noisy in the morning. She always woke Michelle up. Sometimes she would even yank off Michelle's covers.

Michelle sighed as she began to get dressed. It was kind of lonesome with nobody around. Hurrying downstairs, she thought that maybe she and Stephanie could patch things up over breakfast.

But her sister wasn't in the kitchen. "Where's Stephanie?" she asked her dad.

Danny flipped some blueberry pancakes onto her plate. "She said she had to get to school early. Darcy's mom gave her a ride."

Michelle frowned down at her plate. She really missed her sister—and it had been only one day!

I wish I could get her to move back, Michelle thought.

"Better eat up," Danny said. "The bus will be here soon."

Michelle took a bite of her pancakes. How long would Stephanie be mad at her? she wondered.

All day at school, Michelle thought about the big argument with her sister. What should she do? Would Stephanie get tired of sleeping on the couch?

Maybe I should just leave things alone, Michelle thought. Maybe then it'll all just blow over. Maybe Stephanie wasn't even mad anymore! That happened sometimes with silly fights.

But what if she *is* still mad? Maybe I should do something to fix it, Michelle thought.

After school Michelle hurried to her room. One by one, she pulled down all the little signs she had made and threw them in the trash. Then she pulled up the tape that divided the room.

I'll save up my allowance to pay for the ruined T-shirt, too, Michelle decided.

At last she heard Stephanie's bus outside. She heard her sister come inside the house.

Michelle practiced what she would say. She wanted to apologize to Stephanie just right. Then she headed downstairs.

She found her sister sitting on the couch watching TV. "Hi, Stephanie."

Stephanie didn't answer.

Bad news, Michelle thought. She's still angry at me.

Michelle took a deep breath and plunged ahead. "I'm really sorry about everything," shc said quietly.

Stephanie still didn't answer.

Maybe I said it too quietly for her to hear me over the TV. Michelle tried again. "Stephanie, I'm—"

Stephanie jumped up and stared down at Michelle. "Can't I even watch TV without you bothering me?"

"But, Stephanie, please, listen—"

"Leave me alone," Stephanie said, turning her

head. "I'm not talking to you anymore." With that, she stomped into the kitchen and scrawled something on the family message board.

A few seconds later . . . *slam!* The back door banged shut.

Michelle ran into the kitchen and read Stephanie's message: DAD—GONE TO DARCY'S. HOME BY 6:00. STEPHANIE

Oh, no! Stephanie wasn't talking to her. She didn't even want to be in the same room with her!

Michelle grabbed the phone and called her friends. Cassie and Mandy would know what to do.

"Let me get this straight," Mandy said later, looking around Michelle's room. "Your sister has moved out to the couch. You get this whole cool room to yourself. But you want us to help you figure out a way to make her move *back?*"

Michelle nodded.

"Sorry, Michelle," Mandy said. "I think you're nuts!"

Cassie giggled. "But Michelle's right," she said. "It can be lonely to have your own room. I love when you guys sleep over."

Mandy flopped down on her back on Stephanie's bed. She let her head hang over the edge. Her long dark curly hair dangled to the floor. "I'd give anything to have a great big room like this all to myself."

"Come on, you guys," Michelle said. "What am I going to do?"

Cassie picked up a perfume bottle from Stephanie's dresser and sprayed some in the air. "P.U.!" she exclaimed, wrinkling her nose. "Maybe you can buy Stephanie a present— like some perfume that doesn't stink!"

"I've already made this for her birthday." Michelle showed them the special throw pillow she sewed for Stephanie's bed. "Do you think she'll be surprised?"

"Definitely," Mandy said, taking the pillow.

"You did a nice job," Cassie added. "It's not bad for homemade."

Michelle's heart sank. "I don't think it's a big enough surprise to make her like me again."

"But what else can you do?" Cassie asked. "Give her another present?"

Michelle shook her head.

"Too bad you can't throw her a surprise party or something," Mandy said.

"Yeah," Michelle said glumly.

The girls stared silently at the pillow.

"Wait a minute." Michelle raised her head. "Who says I can't?"

"Who says you can't what?" Cassie asked.

"Throw her a surprise party," Michelle said excitedly. "For her birthday!"

Mandy sat up on Stephanie's bed. "By yourself?"

Michelle thought about it. Should she ask Dad and D.J. to help? Uncle Jesse and Aunt Becky and the twins? And Joey?

No, Michelle decided. To make Stephanie like her again, she had to do this without her family. But that didn't mean Cassie and Mandy couldn't help!

The three friends began to make plans. Michelle found a pad of paper in her desk drawer. "Mandy, you take notes."

Mandy uncapped a pen and got ready to write.

"Let's see," Michelle said. "I'll invite about five of Stephanie's friends—and our family, of course."

Michelle picked up Stephanie's address book from her night table. Michelle knew her sister wouldn't want her going through it. But how else could she get the addresses she needed?

She opened it up and placed it on the floor. Then she got out some art materials.

Michelle and Cassie wrote out the invitations. Mandy began to make decorations and posters out of colored paper.

Michelle stacked the invitations into a pile. "The most important thing is to keep this party a secret," she reminded her friends.

"Secret? What secret?" someone asked as the door was opened.

Michelle gasped. It was Stephanie!

Chapter

6

♡   Michelle jumped up. She slammed the
door in Stephanie's face. She couldn't let her
sister see the decorations and invitations for
the party!

"Michelle!" Stephanie shouted. "Open the
door!"

"Quick," Michelle whispered to her friends.
"Hide the party stuff!"

Michelle held the door while Cassie and
Mandy shoved the invitations and decorations
into a shopping bag.

"Michelle!" Stephanie hollered. "Let me in!"

Michelle tried to stall her. "Uh, I thought you weren't staying here anymore. . . ."

"If you don't open this door right now, I'll tell Dad!"

Michelle glanced around quickly. Was everything put away? "The pillow!" She gasped.

Cassie soccer-kicked it under Michelle's bed.

"Michelle!" Stephanie banged on the door. "Let me in!"

Michelle opened the door. "Sorry," she told Stephanie. "I guess the door was stuck."

Stephanie raised an eyebrow as if she didn't believe her. Then she said, "Listen. I was thinking. This fight we've been having. It's pretty silly, and I—"

Stephanie stared down at the floor.

Michelle followed her gaze. Oh, no! Stephanie's address book was lying open on the rug.

Stephanie snatched it up. "Michelle, what were you doing with this?"

"Uh, nothing. Really." Michelle glanced nervously at the shopping bag on the floor.

"What are you hiding in there, Michelle?" Stephanie picked up the bag. "Some more of my stuff?"

"No way," Michelle said, quickly snatching it up.

"Uh, Mandy, Cassie, I think it's time for you guys to go," Michelle said, pushing them toward the door.

"You're right," Mandy agreed.

"Don't forget the, uh . . . your stuff," Michelle blurted out. She shoved the shopping bag full of party things into Cassie's hands. Then she followed them downstairs to the front door. "And don't forget to mail the invitations," she whispered to her friends.

The girls nodded and quickly left.

Michelle was just about to close the door, when Stephanie came stomping down the stairs with a backpack. "Stephanie, I—"

But her sister flew past her so fast, Michelle couldn't explain. She couldn't even say, "I'm sorry."

"I'm going to Darcy's house," Stephanie yelled. "At least *she* won't go through my stuff the minute I turn my back!"

Michelle stood in the doorway and watched her sister rush down the walkway. Boy, Stephanie is madder than ever, she thought. This party better work!

Chapter

7

♥ "Nicky, would you please tell Michelle to pass the salt?" Stephanie said the next morning at breakfast.

Michelle and everyone else at the table stared at Stephanie. Her manners were perfect. But her request was kind of weird.

After all, she was sitting right next to Michelle.

Michelle felt everyone staring at her and squirmed.

Nicky pulled on the sleeve of Michelle's

T-shirt. "Hey! Stephanie told me to tell you to pass her the salt."

Michelle turned to Stephanie. "Why can't you just ask me yourself?" she said.

"Nicky," Stephanie answered sweetly. "Please tell your cousin Michelle that I'm not talking to her. And she knows why."

"Stephanie says she's not talking to you!" Nicky hollered at Michelle. "And you know why."

Michelle knew why, all right. But she had to look in Stephanie's address book. She needed to know where Stephanie's friends lived. For the surprise party. "But, Steph—" Michelle began.

Stephanie's eyes flashed. "Nicky, *please* tell *Michelle* that if *she's* going to be so *rude—*"

Michelle tightened her lips. Her sister was *really* taking this business of not talking to her way too far!

"No," Michelle said to Nicky, "tell *Stephanie* that if she's going to be so *weird—*"

Nicky's blond head whipped back and forth between the two sisters.

"Weird!" Stephanie exclaimed. "Nicky, please tell *her I'm* not the one who's *weird. She's* the one who—"

"Nicky," Michelle interrupted, *"please* tell *Stephanie* that—"

"Hold it right there!" Danny Tanner exclaimed. His chair screeched on the kitchen floor as he stood up.

Everyone stopped talking and stared at Danny. Michelle couldn't remember the Tanner breakfast table ever being this quiet.

Danny patted his mouth with his napkin, then cleared his throat. In a calm, quiet voice, he said, "Stephanie. Michelle. Would one of you girls *please* tell me what's going on?"

Aunt Becky laughed a nervous laugh and

stood up. "Um, Nicky, Alex, come on. Let's go brush your teeth." She helped the boys down from their chairs. "You, too, Jesse."

"But I'm still eating!" Uncle Jesse protested.

"No problem." Aunt Becky picked up his breakfast plate and led him out of the room.

The twins scooted out after their parents.

Joey scooped the rest of his scrambled eggs onto a piece of toast. "Great takeout, Danny," he joked as he left the room.

D.J. quickly finished her juice. "This is one family event I don't want to attend." She grabbed her backpack and left.

Michelle sank back into her seat. She wished everyone had stayed.

"Now," Danny said. "What's going on between you two girls?"

Stephanie shot a glance at Michelle. "It's all

Michelle's fault, Dad," Stephanie blurted out. "She's making my life miserable!"

Michelle started to protest, but Danny held up his hand. "Stephanie, can you explain more clearly what you mean?"

"Easy!" Stephanie replied. "She never lets me have any privacy. And she's always going through all my stuff. First she read my private birthday card. Then she stole the new paints I got for school—"

"Borrowed," Michelle insisted.

"If you take it without asking, I call it stealing," Stephanie declared. She turned back to her father. "And then yesterday Michelle held the door closed and wouldn't let me in our room. And do you know what I found when I went in?"

"What?" Danny asked.

"Michelle and her friends were snooping through my private address book!"

Danny looked shocked. "Michelle wouldn't—" he started to say.

"Yes, she would, Dad!" Stephanie interrupted. "I *caught* her."

Michelle felt her father's eyes on her.

Respecting someone's privacy was one of his strictest rules. It had to be in such a full house.

"Michelle," he said slowly. "Is this true?"

Michelle gulped. It *was* true. And Michelle knew she was in trouble. But if she explained everything to Dad, Stephanie's surprise would be totally ruined.

What should I do? she wondered.

Chapter

8

♥ "Is this true?" Danny repeated. "Did you look in Stephanie's address book?"

Michelle took a deep breath. "Well, uh . . . yes," she admitted.

"Why?" Danny asked.

Michelle glanced at Stephanie, then back at her father. She didn't know what to say. She didn't want to spoil Stephanie's surprise birthday party. "I can't tell you," she said at last.

Her father sighed. He did not look happy. "Okay, Michelle. We'll have a talk later."

Stephanie grinned.

"Stephanie, you're excused," Danny said. "Michelle, will you help me clear the table, please?"

"Sure, Dad." Michelle got up and started stacking plates.

When she finished clearing the dishes from the table, Danny told her to wait in the living room for him.

Sadly Michelle went into the living room. She pulled a family album off the shelf and sat down on the couch. She flipped through the pages. Nearly every page had a photo of Michelle and Stephanie.

Michelle and Stephanie dressed up as Mickey and Minnie Mouse on Halloween one year.

Michelle and Stephanie clowning around at the beach.

Michelle and Stephanie sharing a tent on a camping trip.

Sure we had our ups and downs, like all sisters, but we used to be so close, Michelle thought. Now everything is all messed up. Maybe I should just tell Stephanie about the party. Maybe that will make things all right again.

Danny came in then and saw her looking at the album. He sat down beside her. "Oh, look. There's you and Stephanie on your third birthday." He chuckled. "When you were little, Stephanie wouldn't let you out of her sight."

"Really?" Michelle asked.

Danny nodded. "Now, do you want to tell me about this address-book thing with Stephanie?"

Michelle sighed. Guess I'd better tell him the truth.

"I was going through Stephanie's address book because I needed addresses for some of her friends," she replied.

"But I don't understand," Danny said. "Why didn't you just ask Stephanie? And why do you need addresses for *her* friends?"

"Because," Michelle explained, "I was trying to plan a party for her birthday on Tuesday. And I wanted it to be a surprise."

Danny looked stunned. "You were planning a surprise birthday party for your sister? All by yourself?"

Michelle nodded. Was she in trouble for that?

"Oh, Michelle." Her father gave her a big hug. "I think that's the sweetest thing," he said with a delighted smile.

"Really?" Michelle asked, surprised.

"Really," Danny said. "I think it's absolutely terrific."

Michelle was so relieved! "It was the only way I could think of to make Stephanie like me again," she explained.

"Stephanie still likes you," Danny assured her. "She's your sister. She loves you."

"Not right now," Michelle said sadly. "And I guess I can't blame her."

Danny shook his head. "This is all part of growing up with sisters. Working things out. Learning how to get along with others. Especially two sisters who have to share a room. That's not always easy—for anybody."

Michelle smiled. Her dad *did* understand!

"And you know what?" he added. "I think this party will be just the thing to make you two best friends again."

"I hope so," Michelle replied.

"I'm really glad you told me," Danny said.

"You are?"

"Sure," Danny said with a smile. "Because I'm just the person to help you plan the party. Now," Danny said. "What about invitations?"

"Cassie and Mandy and I already made them," Michelle reported.

"What about decorations?" he asked.

"Done."

"Food?"

"Already planned," Michelle said. "We're going to have a make-your-own ice cream sundae bar."

"What a great idea!" Danny said. He shook his head. "I'm so proud of my little girl. It sounds like you're doing a great job all by yourself."

"Thanks, Dad." Michelle beamed with pride.

"So, what's your plan to get Steph to the party?" he asked.

Plan?

Uh-oh. Michelle forgot all about that!

The surprise party is in three days, Michelle thought in a panic. I need a plan—and quick!

Chapter

9

♡ "Hey, what's all this ice cream for?" Stephanie asked when she opened the freezer. It was Tuesday—Stephanie's birthday. The day of her big surprise party. "Is somebody having a party or something?"

"Don't touch that!" Michelle shouted as she ran toward the freezer. Her dad had bought the ice cream the night before.

Stephanie glared at Michelle. "*If* I were talking to you—which I'm *not*—I'd ask you why not?"

"Because," Michelle said. "It's for . . ."

Quick! Think of something, she told herself. Why would anybody have that much ice cream in the freezer?

"It's for . . . a science project!" Michelle blurted out.

"What?" Stephanie exclaimed.

"Cassie and Mandy and I are doing a . . . a science project," Michelle replied. "We're testing the, uh . . . freezing and melting points of different ice creams."

Stephanie laughed. "No way."

"Sure," Michelle insisted. "Don't tell me you never thought about it, Stephanie. We're trying to find out things like: Does chocolate melt faster than vanilla? Does frozen yogurt hold up in the hot sun better than ice cream?"

"And Mrs. Yoshida bought this?" Stephanie asked, shaking her head. Mrs. Yoshida was Michelle's fourth-grade teacher.

"She thought it was a super idea," Michelle said, crossing her fingers behind her back.

Stephanie shook her head as she closed the freezer door. "Elementary school sure has changed since I was in fourth grade."

Michelle sighed in relief, and then she grinned. Hey! Stephanie and I are talking again.

She smiled at her sister. But Stephanie had already turned away. She was leaving the kitchen.

Then Michelle remembered something important. She still needed to figure out a way to get Stephanie to the party! Everything she had thought of so far was lame.

I have to say something to her, Michelle thought. I have to say something right now! "Uh, wait—Stephanie?"

Stephanie stopped and sighed impatiently. "What?"

Whoa, Michelle thought. Stephanie was as cool as an ice cream sundae again. "I, uh, need you to come home this afternoon right after school."

"Why?" Stephanie asked.

"Because," Michelle said. What could she say? She had to be careful not to give anything away about the party. "Because you have to . . . help me clean up our room."

"Why should I?" Stephanie demanded. "It's not really my room anymore."

Michelle started to panic. What if Stephanie didn't show up to her own surprise birthday party?

"Because Dad said to." Michelle crossed her fingers again. I hope my fingers don't get stuck like this, she thought.

Stephanie shrugged. "I'll think about it."

Now Michelle was really worried. "You'd better just do it."

"*You'd* better just *not* tell me what to do," Stephanie snapped. Then she stormed out of the room.

Michelle plunked down at the kitchen table. She glanced out the window at the sunny sky. She knew the stars were always up there—even in the daytime when you couldn't see them.

Could you still wish on a star if you couldn't see it? Michelle wondered. Well, it's worth a try, she told herself.

Then she wished with all her heart that Stephanie would please show up for the party!

At school that day Stephanie's surprise party was all Michelle could think about.

Mrs. Yoshida had to ask Michelle twice to spell the word *miracle*. "Miracle," Michelle said. "M-i-r-a-c-l-e." Then she thought, it would be a *miracle* if the surprise party was perfect.

At lunchtime all she could think about was if she had enough ice cream and toppings.

On the playground she let three strikes zip past because she thought she had forgotten to wrap Stephanie's present!

At last the final bell rang. Cassie and Mandy were going straight home with Michelle. Cassie's mom gave them a ride so they'd get there quicker than by the bus. Michelle giggled excitedly as they squeezed into the car. The backseat was full of helium balloons!

"Thanks for picking these up for me," Michelle told Mrs. Wilkins.

"I was glad to do it," Mrs. Wilkins said with a smile.

They reached the Tanner home. The girls giggled as they carried the bobbing balloons into the house.

"We have to hurry," Michelle told her

friends. "Stephanie's school gets out in forty-five minutes!"

First they tied the birthday balloons all around the room. They looked great! Cassie had brought a roll of crepe paper streamers. They quickly strung them across all the doorways.

Michelle set up a card table in one corner and covered it with one of her father's nicest linen tablecloths. Then she set out bowls and spoons for the ice cream, and some of the toppings that her dad had bought.

"I guess we'll wait till everyone's here before we put out the ice cream," she said.

Mandy helped Michelle tape up the HAPPY BIRTHDAY STEPHANIE banner that Michelle had made.

Then Michelle reached into a shopping bag. She pulled out a poster Mandy had made for all the guests to sign.

Then something else fell out of the bag.

The colorful invitations to Stephanie's birthday party.

"Oh, no!" Michelle cried as they tumbled to the ground. "Nobody mailed the invitations!"

Chapter

10

♥ "Cassie!" Michelle cried. "I thought you mailed the invitations!"

Cassie looked at Mandy. Mandy looked at Cassie.

"I thought *you* mailed them," Cassie said nervously.

"I thought *you* mailed them," Mandy said miserably. "Oh, Michelle! I'm sorry!"

"Me, too," Cassie said.

Michelle felt terrible, but she shook her head. "No, it's *my* fault, too. I stuffed the invitations in the bag. And then I forgot all about them! I should have asked. I should have checked. . . ."

"I feel terrible," Cassie said. "How can we have a party without any guests?"

Mandy and Cassie shook their heads.

Then Michelle had an idea. "Come on. Maybe we can still call everybody."

"Should we look in Stephanie's address book?" Mandy asked.

Michelle shook her head. "No way. I'm not going to do that again." She pulled a heavy phone book out of a drawer.

Michelle sat by the phone while her friends frantically looked up the numbers.

Michelle dialed the first number. She blew her strawberry-blond bangs out of her eyes as she listened to the phone ring.

"Hello . . ."

"Hi!" Michelle said quickly. "This is Michelle Tanner and—"

"We're not home right now, but if you'll leave your name and number, we'll call you as soon as we can. . . ."

"I got an answering machine," she told her friends.

"Leave a message," Mandy said. "Remember, the junior high school kids probably aren't home yet."

"Right!" Michelle waited for the tone, then left her invitation to Stephanie's surprise birthday party.

She hung up. "Quick! Give me another number!"

Cassie called out a number, and Michelle quickly punched the buttons on the phone. "Oooh! Another answering machine!" She waited for the tone, then left a message.

Michelle left four messages. She had one more number to call.

Michelle glanced at her watch. "Stephanie

might be home any minute. Cassie, Mandy, go outside. If you see Stephanie come home, keep her away from the house—just until everybody gets here."

"But how?" Cassie demanded as they headed for the door.

"I don't know," Michelle called out. "You'll think of something!"

At last the phone stopped ringing. "Hello?" a voice said.

A real person! "H-hello!" Michelle said quickly. "This is Michelle Tanner. Can I speak to Allie?"

"Oh, hi, Michelle. This is Allie."

Thank goodness! She was actually talking to one of Stephanie's friends. "I'm calling to tell you about Stephanie's surprise birthday party—"

"Oh, I already know about it," Allie said cheerfully.

Huh? How could she know? Michelle wondered. Did one of Michelle's invitations actually go out?

"Yeah, it was Darcy's idea," Allie went on. "Stephanie was so surprised when we told her we were taking her to Water World for her birthday this afternoon."

Water World? *This* afternoon?

Michelle dropped the phone.

Chapter

11

♥ Michelle picked the receiver up from the floor. "W-W-Water World?" she said into the phone.

"Sure," Allie replied. "Stephanie said it was going to be her best birthday ever."

Michelle closed her eyes and sighed.

"Michelle? Are you still there?" Allie asked.

"Yeah, I'm here."

"So . . ." Allie said. "How come you're calling about it?"

"Uh, well, I—" Michelle didn't know what

to say. "Oh, there's someone at the door. I have to go." She slammed down the phone.

"Surprise," Michelle told herself. "You've planned a party for your sister—and she won't even be there."

Michelle felt like the dumbest, lamest nerd in the world.

Now there was only one thing to do.

Call everybody she'd just called—and tell them to forget about the party!

Michelle felt her face grow hot as she dialed the first number. Luckily she got an answering machine again. So she only had to be stupid on tape, not in person.

Michelle wandered into the living room and stared at all the decorations. The pretty balloons bobbed cheerfully around the room. The table with the bowls and drinks looked so pretty.

What a waste, Michelle thought miserably.

She pulled at one end of a colored paper streamer. I guess I'd better take down the decorations, she thought sadly.

"Stephanie's not here yet," Mandy said, coming through the front door. Then she saw Michelle's face. "What's wrong?"

Michelle stared at her friend. A tear slipped down her cheek. "There's not going to be any party." She told Mandy what happened.

"Oh, no," Mandy said, putting her arm around Michelle's shoulders. "This is awful."

"I know," Michelle said. "And it's all my fault. Now Stephanie's going to be mad at me forever!"

Chapter

12

♥ "I wish I never ever planned this stupid party!" Michelle cried. She ran upstairs to her room. Her very own, *empty* bedroom.

A few minutes later Michelle heard a soft knock on her bedroom door. "Michelle, are you okay? Can I come in?"

"Okay," Michelle said. She wiped the tears from her face. "Where's Mandy?"

Cassie shrugged. "Downstairs, I guess."

"I guess that's where I should be," Michelle said. "Instead of up here crying."

"Yeah. Come on, you'll feel better," Cassie said cheerfully.

Together they went back downstairs.

The sight of the living room decorated for the party almost made Michelle cry again. She started to take down a poster.

"Stop!" Cassie cried.

"But why?" Michelle asked. "Nobody's coming to my dumb party."

"Uh, well, we can still have a party," Mandy said brightly. "It's a shame to waste all the ice cream . . ."

"Yeah, right," Michelle muttered. She didn't want to be rude and tell her friend that was a dumb idea. But it was.

Just then Michelle heard a key in the lock.

"Oh, no! What if it's Stephanie?" she cried.

But when the door opened, Michelle sighed in relief. It wasn't Stephanie. It was her dad.

"I'm sorry I'm late," Danny said as he hurried

inside. He glanced around the room and smiled. "But it looks like you didn't need my help anyway. Michelle, everything looks just wonderful!"

"It doesn't matter," Michelle said.

Danny frowned. "But why? Michelle, what's wrong?"

Michelle told him everything. That no one was coming to the party.

"I know what we can do," Danny said, giving her a hug. "We can still have a surprise party for Steph when she comes home."

"A birthday party with none of her friends?" Michelle asked. "After she's had a wonderful time at Water World?"

"Sure!" Danny said. "Why not?"

Michelle's shoulders sagged. "It's not exactly the big surprise party I had planned."

"It'll be fine," her father insisted. He turned to Cassie and Mandy. "And, of course, you girls are welcome to stay, too."

"Thanks," the girls said.

"Well," Danny said cheerfully. "I guess I'd better go start dinner, huh?" And he went into the kitchen, whistling "Happy Birthday."

How can he be so cheerful? Michelle wondered, her feelings hurt.

"Don't worry, Michelle," Mandy said. "I'm sure the party will be lots of fun."

"Oh, Michelle," her father called out from the kitchen door. "Would you take out the trash for me, please?"

"Now?" Michelle asked.

"Yes, now."

"All right, Dad. I'll be right back," she told her friends.

She shuffled into the kitchen. Danny handed her the bag.

Rolling her eyes, Michelle dragged the bag outside and down the steps to the trash can.

I guess Stephanie's at Water World by now,

she thought as she lifted the lid. She's probably zooming down a super-size water slide.

Michelle slammed the trash bag into the can and plodded back to the house.

She reached for the doorknob and yanked.

"Hey!" The doorknob was stuck. Michelle twisted it and pulled. No luck.

It wasn't stuck. It was locked. She was locked out of the house!

"Hey! Somebody let me in!" she hollered. She banged on the door. She rang the doorbell. But nobody came to the door.

Just my luck, Michelle thought as she went around the side of the house. What *else* can go wrong today?

Chapter

13

♥ Michelle stomped around to the front porch. That door was locked, too. Michelle rang the bell. *Ding-ding-ding-ding!* "Let me in!" she hollered.

The door opened and Michelle walked inside.

"Surprise!"

Michelle nearly jumped a foot.

The room was filled with people: Stephanie, Darcy, Allie, and all of Michelle's friends. Her whole family was there, too.

"What's going on?" Michelle gasped.

Stephanie ran over and threw her arms around Michelle.

Now Michelle was totally confused!

"I asked Dad about the ice cream. He told me everything," Stephanie said. "He didn't want me to be mad at you anymore. And then I had a great idea—to throw a surprise party for *you!*"

Everyone in the room clapped and cheered.

Michelle looked at Cassie and Mandy. "Did you guys know about this?" she asked with a smile.

Her two best friends grinned back at her and nodded.

"But it's not my birthday!" Michelle said.

"Who cares?" Stephanie said. "It was so nice of you to throw a surprise party for me. I decided to have some fun and surprise you right back! Look," she added, dragging Michelle into the room. "We've got pizza, drinks, music—the works. You already did the decorations. . . ." Stephanie laughed. "And the science experiment."

"The what?"

"The ice cream, silly!"

Michelle laughed. "Oh, yeah. But, Steph," Michelle said. "What about Water World?"

"We're taking her to Water World Saturday," Darcy explained.

"It'll be more fun to spend all day there," Allie added.

"And you're invited," Stephanie told Michelle. "Do you want to bring Cassie and Mandy?"

"You bet!" Michelle cried.

"Hey, come on, you guys," Joey said. "Let's eat! I want to get to that wonderful make-your-own ice cream sundae bar."

"Only if you eat all your vegetables," Danny teased.

"No problem," Stephanie said, flipping open a pizza box. "Because tonight the veggies are on pizza!"

Everyone had a great time. The make-your-own ice cream sundae bar was a big hit. And some of the weird combinations actually looked like science experiments!

Later, at bedtime, Michelle sat in her bed, waiting for Stephanie to show up.

"Hey, kiddo, I'm moving back in," Stephanie announced. She dragged her quilt and pillow into the room. *"If* that's okay."

"Okay?" Michelle said. "It's great!" She smiled shyly. "And, Steph, I really missed you."

"Me, too, squirt." Stephanie flopped down on her bed. "This is so much more comfortable than the couch!"

Both girls giggled.

"I'm really sorry I used your stuff without

asking," Michelle went on. "And I promise I'll never do it again."

"I'm sorry, too," Stephanie said. "I know I sometimes act like this is my room and you're the visitor. But I'd rather share. It was hard to go to sleep without your snoring!"

"*My* snoring!" Michelle cried. "You're the one who snores!"

Stephanie laughed and tossed a pillow Michelle's way.

That reminded her. She still hadn't given Stephanie her special birthday present. She stuck her head under the bed and pulled out the pretty wrapped package.

"Here, Steph," Michelle said. She handed her sister the gift. "Happy birthday."

"A party *and* a present, too?" Stephanie exclaimed. "Michelle, you didn't have to do that."

"I know," Michelle said. "But I wanted to."

Stephanie crossed her legs on her bed and carefully opened the gift. When she saw what was inside, her eyes lit up.

It was the ruffly throw pillow Michelle had made for her bed. Written in the middle, in glitter paint, were the words HOME SWEET HOME.

"Did you make this yourself?" Stephanie asked.

Michelle nodded.

"I love it." She gave Michelle a hug. "And I love you, too."

Later, when Stephanie turned out the lights, everything felt right again.

Michelle giggled when she heard her sister snoring softly from the other side of the room.

Then she glanced out her window at the stars. But she didn't need to make any more wishes. Everything was perfect just the way it was.

FULL HOUSE™

SISTERS

A brand-new series starring Stephanie AND Michelle!

#1 Two On The Town

Stephanie and Michelle find themselves
in the big city—and in big trouble!

#2 One Boss Too Many

Stephanie and Michelle think camp will be major fun.
If only these two sisters were getting along!

When sisters get together...expect the unexpected!

A MINSTREL® BOOK

Published by Pocket Books

2012-01

FULL HOUSE Stephanie™

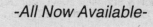

FULL HOUSE™
Michelle

A MINSTREL® BOOK
Published by Pocket Books

Simon & Schuster Mail Order Dept. BWB

200 Old Tappan Rd., Old Tappan, N.J. 07675

Please send me the books I have checked above. I am enclosing $_____(please add $0.75 to cover the postage and handling for each order. Please add appropriate sales tax). Send check or money order--no cash or C.O.D.'s please. Allow up to six weeks for delivery. For purchase over $10.00 you may use VISA: card number, expiration date and customer signature must be included.

Name _____

Address _____

City _____ State/Zip _____

VISA Card # _____ Exp.Date _____

Signature _____

1033-30